Buddy   Max   Spot   Spike

For Ezzy and Levon
—J.H.

Build, Dogs, Build: A Tall Tail
Copyright © 2014 by James Horvath
All rights reserved. Manufactured in China.
No part of this book may be used or reproduced in any manner whatsoever without
written permission except in the case of brief quotations embodied in critical articles
and reviews. For information address HarperCollins Children's Books, a division of
HarperCollins Publishers, 10 East 53rd Street, New York, NY 10022.
www.harpercollinschildrens.com

Library of Congress Cataloging-in-Publication Data is available.
ISBN 978-0-06-218967-7 (trade bdg.)–ISBN 978-0-06-218968-4 (lib. bdg.)

The artist used Adobe Illustrator to create the digital illustrations for this book.
Design by Martha Rago. Hand-lettering by James Horvath.
13 14 15 16 17 SCP 10 9 8 7 6 5 4 3 2 1
❖
First Edition

James Horvath

Build, Dogs, Build

A Tall Tail

HARPER
An Imprint of HarperCollinsPublishers

EXIT

DIG DOGS

DUKE

Get moving, crew.
We're heading downtown.
An old building there
needs to come down.

Time to get rolling.
Duke just got a call.
Load up the bulldozer
and big wrecking ball.

Here's the building,
all crumbled and cracked.
We'll knock it down quickly
with a couple of whacks.

The crane is in place.
The angle's correct.

Get the ball swinging now.

Wreck, dogs, wreck!

With a *BOOM* the ball
sails right through the wall.
Stand clear now—
the building is starting to fall.

The bulldozer clears away
piles of rubble, and

bricks and concrete
without any trouble.

The dump truck hauls off
load after load.
Fill it to the top,
then head down the road.

Quick work, dogs.
The site is all clear.
Now set up the barricades
and unpack the gear.

MENU

HOT DOG
JUMBO DOG
CORN DOG
CHEESE DOG
CHILI DOG
VEGGIE DOG

R COACH

Grab a fast snack
from the dog in the van
while Duke the foreman
double-checks the plan.

Start digging trenches
to run all the pipes
for water and drains,
many sizes and types.

Head down in the tunnel
to secure the connection.
And be sure it runs
in the proper direction!

Grab shovels and rakes—
there's concrete to pour.
This building is going
to need a good floor.

Yard after yard
is poured into place.
Ten inches thick
is a mighty strong base.

Here comes the steel!
Unload it right here.
Ton after ton
builds tier after tier.

These giant red girders
look exactly the same.
Let's weld them together
and build a tall frame.

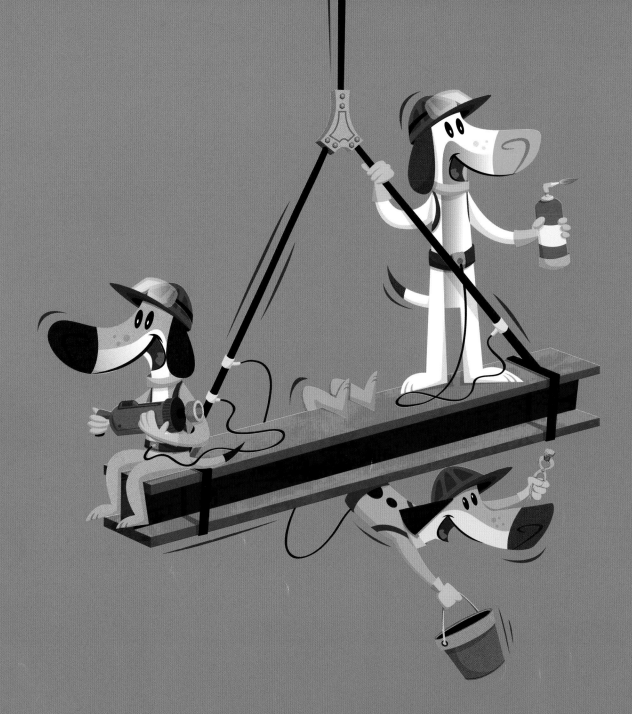

The iron team is working–
a high-flying breed–
welding and riveting
with great skill and speed.

Look out, dogs!

Watch out for that glass!

Oh no, too late.

The truck's gonna crash!

Balls bouncing up.
Balls bouncing down.
Balls, balls, balls
flying all over town!

Let's take a quick break
and a well-deserved stretch.
While we gather the balls, we can

fetch, dogs, fetch!

BIG BOUNCE
BALL COMPANY

The excitement is over,
and we've all had fun.
But there are still miles of pipes
and wires to run.

Electricians, plumbers,
and carpenters too–

each one of them has
his own job to do.

This building is bare,
with strong steel for bones.
We'll need mortar and bricks,
concrete and stones.

The beams go up fast,
building room upon room.
As the pumper pumps
liquid cement through its boom.

This crew is the best,
each dog highly skilled.

Let's keep going higher.

Build, dogs, build!

The windows are lifted
and swung through the air,
then fastened and fitted
and set with great care.

The finish work starts.
There's more to install.
Windows and stairs,
ceilings and walls.

Lights and fixtures
and doors to pass through,
kitchens and bedrooms
and a bathtub or two.

In comes the paint team
to color the walls.
Red for the doors
and blue for the halls.

The building is finished.
It turned out quite swell.

The last thing to do
is install the doorbell.

The penthouse is perfect,
complete with a view.
There's even a terrace
with a pool for the crew.

The Pethouse

Great job, dogs!
Our work is all through.
Tomorrow we're off.
There's a new job to do.

DuKE   Roxy   Buddy   Max